SCORIA

SCORIA
Short prose from the cinder cone

Kathy Derrick and Jac Jenkins

Pavlova Press

A catalogue record for this book is available from the
National Library of New Zealand.

ISBN 978-0-473-50065-8

First published in 2019 by
Pavlova Press NZ
PO Box 706, Kerikeri
New Zealand
www.pavlovapress.co.nz

© Kathy Derrick & Jac Jenkins 2019
The moral rights of the authors have been asserted.

With the exception of 'Advance of the Cane Toads' and 'Scales', the pieces in *Scoria* are fiction.

This book is copyright. Apart from fair dealing for the purpose of review, private study or research, as permitted under the Copyright Act, no part may be stored or transmitted in any form by any process without permission in writing from the publishers.

Edited by Michelle Elvy
Cover design by Keely O'Shannessy
Typesetting and internal design by CVD Limited

Printed by Your Books, New Zealand

For Hilary, Kate, Justine and Emily

*...my heart was volcanic
as the scoriac rivers that roll...*
—EDGAR ALLAN POE—

Contents

INTRODUCTION
    Bubbles and fragments   3

PRELUDE
    The girl in the drop-hem dress,
        whose mother is stung by a bee   6

ARRHYTHMIA
Sunrise	10
Pōhutukawa	12
Yellow	14
Tulips and chimneys	16
Coffee date	18
Ends and means	19
Flat shoes are made for walking	20
Winter in Alaska	22
While the moon howls	23
Joel's knickers	24
No pleasing Theresa	26
He loves me, he loves me not	28
Virtuoso	29
Staying in bed	30
The good intentions of angels	31
Shoe museum	34
On a cerulean day	35
Self-portrait in the style of Juan Gris	36

Anonymous in a fiction of bricks 38
Salutation 40
Perigee 41
Daughters of the air 42

SEVERANCE
The possum hunt 44
Held fast 45
Settlement 46
Aren't caped crusaders bulletproof? 48
Leaving here 49
Le jour du jugement—Toulon 1793 50
Serving a subpoena in the outback 51
The truth of it 52
The bridge on a rainy Tuesday night 54
Advance of the cane toads 56
Saving Daisy 57
BREAKING: Powerful quake jolts Kermadecs 58
Come with me to Dunkirk 59
Scales: An assimilation of Val Plumwood 60

ELASTICITY
- Stigmeology — 63
- The auburn trail — 64
- When plump berries fall — 71
- Rationalists wear square hats — 72
- Towards apostasy — 74
- My father bought an apple orchard — 76
- Making our way home — 78
- The ghost of my father — 80
- Mount Alpha — 81
- A dog called Mana — 82
- The theory of elasticity — 83
- Slang — 91
- The ticket — 92
- Duchesses don't cry — 94
- Thin places — 95
- Use three-dimensional characters — 96

Notes — 98
Acknowledgements — 103

INTRODUCTION

Bubbles and fragments

Sisters as well as writers, we grew up under the cinder cone mountain of Maungatapere. When active, cinder cones eject basaltic lava which traps gases and solidifies into scoria rock; as a result, scoria is composed of small bubbles and glassy fragments. It is strikingly coloured and has high strength for its weight. Here, in short prose, we examine the small bubbles and glassy fragments of the human condition. This collection is collaborative in the true sense of the word; no piece in its current form is without input from the other.

PRELUDE

The girl in the drop-hem dress, whose mother is stung by a bee

It is near noon in the orchard and small passions of petals are bursting spring into the air.

Or perhaps it's mid-afternoon, hot, and a floral schoolgirl in a drop-hem dress skateboards home from dance class, past the corner dairy with its Coke-red overhang, one muscled calf slightly thicker than the other. At the zebra-crossing she pops the board up and into her grip as she waits for the Merc to cruise to a stop.

Or perhaps it's a sunburnt red Toyota, bonnet blistered and peeling, and there's a Brooklyn Beckham look-alike in the passenger seat with the window open and he winks at her and her heart goes pittity-pattity as she walks the board across the road. She looks back and the driver makes a ring with finger and thumb. She smiles and he pokes a finger in and out in and out in and out.

Or perhaps the girl is a dreadlocked surfer dude and the driver goes *chur, bro*.

Or perhaps the dreadlocked surfer dude is on his longboard and the waves go *churrr, churrr, churrr* as he goes down and under, burning his back on the sand.

Or perhaps there's no surf, it's a deep-ocean drug dream and he's levitating on the crests, black expanding to starry night, and we abandon him to billow and roll.

Perhaps it doesn't happen like that.

Out of the first bloom comes a bee. A woman, ungrey in her fifties, barefoot in the orchard, is stung and rushed to hospital.

Or perhaps she goes on holiday, cycling north, saddle bags filled with jars of jam. She loses her Thermacore shirt, her reading glasses, her black bra. The glasses reappear between a puppy's teeth, and the clothes in her mother-in-law's hall cupboard six weeks later.

Or perhaps she is blind, a blind man, a blindfolded blind man on a dark horse, lurching down the slopes of Manaia with a sack on his head, thinking *I'd be pleased to see the bottom about now*, but there's only a river flowing black behind the stars to guide him, and his knees hold tight to the horse's dark and bare back.

Or the horse is a dirt-bike being fast-ridden by a girl in a drop-hem dress, spring bursting on all sides, and she's calling out a name.

This is not how the story is supposed to go.

ARRHYTHMIA

Sunrise

We'd taken three months off work to rebuild, consolidate, perhaps make that baby we said we wanted.

"Let's drive round Australia," you said.

It seemed like a good idea, so we flew into Perth and headed for Cervantes. I walked among the limestone pillars and cried, my whole body aching with the land. You laughed.

"Let's drive the Gunbarrel Highway," you said. "You want to go to Ayers Rock—we'll get there faster."

"We've got three months," I said. "Can't we take our time?"

"Life's too short to take our time."

The next day we turned east and drove to Wiluna, picked up our permits, stocked up on food and water, and swapped our Daihatsu for a Land Rover.

We arrived at Uluru five days later in the rain, the earth full of flavour, its scent tangy and damp. You ran from one photo stop to the next. I wandered, my collar turned up. Rivulets cascaded down rock faces, springing from nowhere and dashing sideways with no apparent cause.

That was yesterday. This morning the rain has gone and I leave you sleeping to watch the sun rise. The sky writes me a story—pink-threaded words on deep-purple velvet.

You join me, yawning as if you are swallowing the day.

"Let's go to Alice Springs," you say.

"I'd like to stay."

You scowl, collect your pack from the cabin and throw it into the Land Rover. The engine turns over. You won't wait for me.

And I won't leave.

Pōhutukawa

Nick left at dawn. Not wanting to return to our empty bed, I went outside and lay down on the carpet of red stamens coating our sea-front lawn. I watched the sun rise, and as it crept higher, closed my eyes against the rays piercing my pōhutukawa umbrella.

Stamens continued to fall, tickling my nose, my eyelids, my bare arms and legs. I left them where they landed and wondered how long I'd have to lie there before I also became cloaked in red.

I heard the car return, and a few minutes later felt Nick lie down beside me.

"You were gone a long time," I said without opening my eyes.

"I'm always slower at the market without you," he said. "I never know which lettuce to get or if the avocados are ripe." He paused. "You could come with me next time."

"Not yet."

We lay in silence.

"The doctor says we can try again. That there's no reason why …"

"Not yet."

More stamens fell.

"Please, Tara, let me in."

I turned my head away. "Not yet."

Soon we'd both be buried beneath a crimson blanket. A raft of stamens floated down my cheek in the wake of a tear. His hand reached for mine. I started to pull away then stopped. Skin to skin, I let our little fingers rest together for a moment.

Yellow

Neither the Pure Fiji lemongrass natural insect repellent nor my dhal flatulence repels these yellow-striped mosquitoes. You and I punctuate our conversation with flat-handed full stops.

"Have a look at this river-raft trip here, near Sigatoka." *SLAP*.

"Too expensive." *SLAP SLAP*.

I am simply branding myself with handprints—there is no gratification. And there will be no river rafting.

The dhal was inexpensive and rich with coriander. Cloudy yellow. Reverberant. I want more.

You want more from me. Your midnight question still hovers like those yellow-striped bastards. Any one of my answers will brand you with my handprint.

The Fijian bananas are small and luscious. Their brindled skin tears easily from the flesh. We share one for dessert. Caramelised. The ice-cream it came with melted immediately. Sweet enough alone, anyhow.

You tell me the tiger mosquito's stripes are not yellow—that I like to think they are but they're really white. *SLAP*. I nod and study another raised welt on my thigh.

You will anoint my welts with calamine, and as you dab the one on my thigh you will ask me again. I will fade into the sheets, camouflaged.

I order a Natadola Wallbanger. The sole waitress brings it on a tray, flat on the palm of one hand. It is in a tall, dewy glass and tastes of pineapple jellybeans. I drink too fast in the sudden, clumsy silence, spilling a trickle down my chin.

Later in the bure I lie cast within a lagoon-blue spin, canary blennies swimming anticlockwise against the flow. You ask me again. I brand you with my answer.

Tulips and chimneys

The day you burned my book began with a sneeze. Nothing unusual—I always wake with a sneeze poised in my nostrils, like a greyhound waiting for the starting box to open. Well, the starting box had opened and I was ready for the day.

It was light for a June morning, but my breath glittered, and ice rimed the curtainless window. Our shared bohemian dream, romantic in its conception, turned icier by the day. But the sex was still full of heat and gluttony, and I had my first-edition E. E. Cummings' *Tulips and Chimneys* for restoration of faith. "Utter nonsense," you would joke as you flicked through your not-so-glossy car magazines.

I got up to pee. The old toilet had once been an outhouse, but your grandfather had cobbled together an internal access from the lounge. Wrapped in the quilt and barefoot, I scuttled down the hall from worn rug to worn rug, hoping that you'd already lit the fire.

You were sitting on the red-vinyl back seat of your first Falcon, reading *Autocar*. There was an impotent fire, not much more than a glow. Ah well, I would pee and return for a snuggle. As you turned and flashed your one-sided smile at me, I saw the torn page on the hearth—

> *… while on faint hills do frailly go*
> *The peaceful terrors of the snow,*
> *and before your dead face*
> *which sleeps …*

I grabbed the fire tongs and plucked out the scorched remnants of my faith.

Coffee date

We shake hands (firm, smooth) and sit at an outside table (smoker). You undo the buttons on your sports jacket (hmm, slightly weightier than suggested), reach into your breast pocket and hand me Dutch liquorice wrapped in tatty foil and lint (thoughtful, yet what *were* you thinking?). I tuck it into my number two handbag as the waitress brings our coffees.

You talk of how the world is winding up to a seismic shift in thinking (ahh, this could be interesting). I sip my coffee from the fine bone-china cup, certain that the chocolate sprinkle is leaving its signature on my upper lip. I dab with my serviette.

You talk of diminishing fuel supplies, a burgeoning need for horsemanship and self-sufficiency (green—sigh, heard it before). I wonder if my teenage daughter is writhing in sweaty sheets with her boyfriend. Listen, you say, how much use will technology be when the trucks are empty, the trains are empty? (Earnestly green.)

You talk of vegetarianism and smile at my dislike of mustard, assuring me that I would love your mustard lamb (egocentric). You talk of music, your recording studio, and my dislike of jazz, assuring me that I would love your jazz collection (preachy, even). You talk of your ex-wife. (You talk of your ex-wife.)

I place my empty, chocolate-smeared cup on its matching saucer and ask, "Did you know that the nipples of the first Barbie dolls were shaved off before they made it to the shop shelves?"

Ends and means

He rolls off me, pulls up his jeans then fumbles for a cigarette.

"Music's stopped," he says.

I don't bother telling him the band had stopped playing while he was thrashing about on top of me. I can feel parts of my back starting to ache where I've been hammered into the ground and it smells like I'm lying in a cowpat. The three-quarter moon hovering above us doesn't make it any more romantic. I lie still and squeeze my pelvic floor muscles tight.

He drags on his cigarette and stares over at the barn. "It's Sam's 30th in three months. Thank God it'll be in a more civilised place than this. You going?"

"Only if I need you."

He looks down at me, frowning.

I smile. "It's all right. I told you, no strings attached." Just like the good old days in high school when he said he respected me while screwing Larissa Biggs behind my back. Or at university when I finally opened my legs to him, not knowing he was fucking every girl in his dorm.

His eyes narrow. "If Amy finds out …"

"She won't." A car engine turns over. "They're starting to leave. You'd better go before she misses you."

He nods and flicks his cigarette butt into the grass. "Later," he says, standing up.

I lie where he left me, place a hand on my belly and raise my knees.

Flat shoes are made for walking

Midnight collected in alleyways and seeped around corners to claim the wet streets. I shivered under the bus shelter—he was late. A car slowed and stopped long enough for a girl in heels and a miniskirt to leap in, then it roared off, running a red light. I scuffed my sensible flats on the pavement and pulled my coat tighter. Five more minutes then I'd take the bus.

My chunky Nokia vibrated in the pocket of my jeans. I slipped my hand between coat buttons and tugged it out.
running late dropping off ollie 30min?

Fuck! Still, he'd texted me this time at least. Across the road, light fringed the edges of the nightclub door and a bass beat pounded through the wood. Anya would be twerking, flicking her hips as if they were unjointed, the rest of the gang bartering smiles for drinks. The bus slowed down; I waved it on.

A scraggy dog made of bone and shadows rattled out from behind a collection of skips and old boxes. The Nokia vibrated again, almost slipping from my hand as I twitched. I looked at the message.

"Fuck him and his bloody mates!"

I threw the phone into the rubbish bin next to me. It clanged as it ricocheted around the insides.

"Shit." I peered into the dark, plastic-lined recess. It smelt of vomit and last night's chips.

A car screeched to a stop beside me and the girl in high

heels got out, straightening her miniskirt.

The phone blustered at the bottom of the bin. I left it there and stepped out from under the shelter.

Winter in Alaska

The Tuscan scene on my coffee mug reminds me of my dreams. Travis doesn't understand my desire to relax in an Italian courtyard, brave an Alaskan winter or explore the Inca Trail. He has no desire to go anywhere.

I pick up the mug. Warmth infuses my fingers. I close my eyes and press my lips to the outside. Heat floods my body, sends tingles into unexpected places like Travis did last night. He knew when to ask.

"Marry me." Whispered.

"Yes." Breathless.

I take a sip. Bitter but good, the taste lingers.

While the moon howls

He is a writer and a philosopher. I am a beauty therapist, offering cheap skin-treatments to wannabe beauties. We reached for the same apple at the same time at the Bridge Café. That's how it started—with a sharp intake of breath. Five weeks later we exhaled.

He said microdermabrasion would lead him to laugh, the word itself a tickle. I stared and said, "I don't understand. I'm not ticklish."

He spoke of metaphysics, the psychedelics of the universe, the vividness of the unknown. I said, "There's nothing beneath the underneath and space is simply spacious."

He replied, "Space is not a vacuum, but a banquet."

He read aloud what he wrote at night—strings of words like *thirteen hungry ghosts circling a howly moon in a dark sorrow-sky*.

I said, "I've never heard the moon howl."

He said, "It only happens when you sleep."

I left as he slept.

Joel's knickers

After six months' travelling I lost my suitcase on the journey home. Three weeks later they told me it had probably been stolen. There wasn't much I missed: my Canon 5D, the authentic Himalayan salt bought from a street vendor in Pakistan, and ten pairs of silk panties designed by my ex-boyfriend, Joel. The camera and salt I replaced, although I suspected the latter wasn't as authentic as the label proclaimed, but my French knickers were irreplaceable.

I first met Joel at a construction site where I was on the engineering team and he worked for Just Like Butter Concrete Cutters. Watching Joel wield his concrete saw made my mouth water and I soon lured him to my bed. In our post-coital glow we'd eat chocolate and watch reruns of *Project Runway*.

One day I came home to find him rummaging through my underwear drawer.

He held out a pair of Warehouse knickers. "Where are your pretty panties?" he asked.

"I don't have any," I said.

So he set about making me some. After a few unsuccessful attempts, he created a pair that could only be described as exquisite. Soon he had numerous designs and an internship with Fashion Central.

When he started sleeping with the models more often than he slept with me, I changed the locks and threw his belongings onto the street—except for the deliciously comfortable ten pairs of panties he'd first designed.

I sure do miss those knickers.

No pleasing Theresa

When Theresa and I got married we said we'd holiday together every year. The first year we stayed in a tiny motel just out of Auckland. Theresa wasn't impressed.

"We'd have better luck squeezing an elephant into a shoebox," she said.

We were out every day but I got variations on the elephant theme each night.

The next year we flew to Wellington. Our unit had a "fully functioning kitchen" that turned out to be a microwave and one hotplate.

"Where's the oven?" she said. "We can't afford to eat out. Ask for a refund."

I bought frozen meals and reheated them while she grumbled about the lack of cooking facilities.

In Taupō we stayed at a lakeside motel with a view.

"Only if you have X-ray vision," she said. "I can't stay here for a week staring at a rooftop."

It was January and every other motel was booked.

"At least it's close to town," I said.

The next year we went to Los Angeles. Our room had breadcrumbs on the bench, cockroaches in the sink and blood on the sheets. Theresa gagged and bolted from the room. I was close behind. We found another hotel, spending two years' worth of holiday money in one hit.

In our fifth year all we could afford was a weekend at the beach and we found a small holiday home on Airbnb. I walked in first and sighed.

"We can find somewhere else," I said.

She pushed past me and, without commenting on the outdated décor or the faded curtains, ran a finger over the bench, stared into the sink and peered under the bedcovers.

"At least it's not Los Angeles," she said and began to unpack her case.

He loves me, he loves me not

Petal. He loves me. *Petal.* In his forging hands I am ductile as copper. *Petal.* I am the blacksmith. *Petal.* Galliano on fire is a sunset on the ocean—it goes down molten. Too many and I am lava, seething down mountains to the water's edge, sizzling to set stone. He collects my scoria pieces for his cactus garden. *Petal.* Tea tastes better from a china pot painted with daisies, a posy in his hand for me. I'm not sorry to have woken him. *Petal.* In the morning, iced water from a tankard strikes my throat like a rapier blade. I leak icicles through my pores. *Petal.* We fence philosophy and theology with buttoned points on our foils, centring our cores before engagement. *Petal.* Rusted apples on the tree practise dying into my hands. *Petal.* Apples pared white and knifed to slices are baked buttersweet and eaten warm, with cream, from one spoon. *Petal.* He wants to bind me—confine me to my high-heeled boots and smooth skin. *Petal.* The sea has painted cirrus on the sand—I walk with him, barefoot on clouds. *Petal.* He has taken his leave of me yet the day won't leave without him. *Petal.* Willingly I leave my body to the science of him. *Petal.* Long into the dark a migraine pounds like a flat tyre thumping tarmac. I hear his rumbling muffler at 2 a.m. *Petal.* We remap our neural pathways with fingertips and tongues. *Petal.* In his hammering hands I am balsa. *Petal.* I build scale models of skyscrapers in which he occupies the penthouse. *Petal.*

Virtuose

I wake to music. A ringtone. Some vaguely familiar classical piece—probably one you played for me once. I lift my head from the white blanket, stiff-necked from the unnatural position. I can't feel my feet on the floor. A nurse in a pallid smock and hot-pink sneakers is thumbing her phone. She shrugs apologetically, pockets the phone, then adjusts your cannula and leaves us.

Your eyelids are closed, lashes almost lost in the swollen folds. Your once-prominent freckles wane in the sallowness of your skin. I see pain sliding its horsehair bow down the bridge of your jaw, and I place my fingertips lightly on the bone to calm the trill. I am now your luthier.

When the tingling in my feet eases I stand, pushing the chair backwards with my legs. You open your eyes at the *screak*. I lean into you and rest my chin in the angle of your neck, pressing my breath into your skin. "Sorry," I whisper. I feel your heart beating in staccato.

Your fingers pluck at the sheet and I pull away from your suffocating heat to take your hand.

Your eyes are rimmed with crusted rheum. Voice dry, you start to tell me about the playlist—Queen's 'Bohemian Rhapsody', Iz's 'Somewhere over the Rainbow' and The Band's 'I Shall Be Released'. Each word you speak is a blue note. I am the mute—I dampen you. My lips are gentle on the scoop of your cheek. I take up the bow and play you until my wrist burns and the soaring end note falls.

Staying in bed

His hand is kneading the curve of her back, coaxing her awake. For a moment she tastes the bitterness of time as slumber reshapes to skin and fingertips. She can't recall his name for a second of dislocation, as if he were a stranger in their bed. She turns under his hand. The sequinned dream-light on the ocean is lost in the waking, but the same spattering stipples his cheek, and his speckled eyes colour themselves greener as his pupils dilate. She quivers under his fingertips as they sketch over her skin and he is drawn onto her.

Later, tucked into the curvature of his body, she hears the thrumming of his blood and imagines herself afloat on his briny swells and furrows. The sun spills a wash of copper and gold over their bodies. He stirs and murmurs. She refocuses on his pulse.

The radio starts with a blare. Jay-Z. She brings her pillow down over her head. He snorts and brings his hand to her breast. "Beyoncé likes him," he says as she pushes his hand aside. He sighs and leaves their bed.

When he brings her coffee she rouses herself from the undertow of somnolence and props herself on the tri-pillow. "Jay-Z is a misogynist and Beyoncé a fool," she says. She doesn't catch his reply as he picks up his work clothes off the floor and heads for the shower.

She sips. Lets the decaf espresso rest on her tongue.

The good intentions of angels

FIELD NOTE #78346: MARCUS AND LAURA
Last month Marcus Posner asked for love. He's lower than slime on a snail's arse and the whole department knows it. But finding love for desperate souls is part of my job description and I had no choice but to accept the case. Laura Compton-Worth, on the other hand, has the sweetest and most captivating soul I've ever seen. Her aura smells of roses and is infused with pink as fresh and delicate as a spring dawn. I never intended for her to meet Marcus and couldn't believe it when I saw them walking hand in hand today. But perhaps I shouldn't be surprised—they do move in similar high-society circles. Note to self—follow up on the Zane Turney situation. I'm sure Laura will love him—softly spoken and a sports-car mechanic. Perfect! Slightly cloudy aura but I blame that on the wife (nasty piece of work).

FIELD NOTE #78435: ZANE AND HIS SOON-TO-BE EX-WIFE
So much for the Laura-Zane idea. I was too focussed on seeing how Zane's separation from his wife panned out that I missed the moment Marcus and Laura took it to the next level. Note to self—check rules regarding free will.

Field Note #78592: Rule number 36
Angels must not impede the free will of humans; however, they may guide the execution of said free will if they believe it is in the human's best interest. Angels are expected to have read parts II, III and IV of the Guidelines. Perfect!

Field note #78593: Zane and Laura and Marcus and Zane's ex-wife
In line with Rule 36, I bumped Zane into Laura and Laura into Zane. I thought I saw a flash of desire in Zane's eyes but it wasn't reciprocated. I even bumped Marcus into Zane's ex—nada. All that effort and now Laura has moved in with Marcus. You know what? If she wants to screw up her own life that's her business but I do have an obligation to find someone for Zane. Note to self—would Samantha Fairley fit the bill?

Field Note #78609: Zane and Samantha and the ex-wife
I've reviewed Samantha Fairley's case notes. She wouldn't normally be my first choice for Zane but she's a reasonable fit. And she's been single for a while now so I need to remove her from my caseload. I was ready to bump them into each other when I found out Zane was back with his wife. I give up. There's an opening in Human Resources, liaising with the minority who can speak with us. I'm going to take the job.

LETTER OF RESIGNATION

Thank you for the opportunity to join the Human Resources department. As instructed, after just one week as consultant to the Sensing Murders team I am tendering my resignation. I thought I knew who killed Laura Compton-Worth so I took matters into my own hands. It turns out I was wrong and for that I unreservedly apologise. I understand there will be no letter of recommendation and that I am required to read *The Guidebook* in full before I can apply for the vacancy in Sanitation.

Shoe museum

Exhibit 359
I haven't worn them in a while, his sneakers on the porch. A funnel of web laces the mouth of the one lying on its side. This is not the City of Marikina, where shoes are shrined to Imelda.

Exhibit 125
I walked out to get the mail in the rain—my small, un-socked feet slopping around. A burr rubbed against my heel.

Exhibit 33
He shook out grass seeds and a small brown skink fell onto the concrete. It scuttled under dry gum leaves cornered in the carport.

Exhibit 2
Sneakers are cheap over there, he said as he unpacked his suitcase on our bed.

On a cerulean day

Ripples lap at my feet, skimming the hem of my cerulean gown. My teenage daughter stands next to me. Mum is sitting on a beach chair, scowling at the sea, the sun, me.

My first wedding had been at the local sports complex. Mum, Rob's mother and his four sisters ignored my tentative suggestions for décor and floral arrangements. My thoughts on food were dismissed as too modern and we had to have a renowned photographer, not my best friend from university who was surplus to bridesmaid requirements.

"Five bridesmaids would be obscene," they said.

A ceremony on the beach was deemed equally ridiculous.

For the dress they chose oyster brocade and a design reminiscent of Lady Di's that hid my sins, while the bridesmaids dressed themselves in peachblow satin. I looked like an albino ostrich flanked by pink flamingos. Rob and I lasted three years.

Today, Tom has my hand in a firm grip as if he'll never let go. I smile up at him and hear the faint click of my best friend's camera. Gulls soar overhead while a kingfisher, perched on a piece of driftwood, stares at us. Tūī reel drunkenly from one flax flower to the next.

The breeze caresses my belly with silk.

Self-portrait in the style of Juan Gris

I don't know what I look like. My world is confined to this hall of carnival mirrors—small screens, magazines, the lenses of your glasses.

LIPS
You like to watch me do my lips—Stripdown liner, Angel lipstick, Turkish Delight gloss. You say Leonard Cohen could draw the hallelujah from lips like that. I don't tell you that they're Kim Kardashian's lips, and that I don't like the taste. I bruise my lids with Purple Obsession and Burning Black to make a point that you miss.

FACE
This morning my face is naked—we overslept. You botched your Windsor knot and asked me to retie it before grabbing your briefcase and running for the train. I take a later one and barely make my kettlebell class.

CORE
The kettlebell instructor demonstrates the squat—she says it's a fantastic way to tighten our pelvic floors. Once she was a nightclub dancer. Now she is a wife and mother. "My pelvic floor is fine," I whisper triumphantly to the wall-to-wall mirror.

***

I don't know what I look like to my patients. They undress themselves by my desk as if they trust me, but they are talking to the doctor that I wear. By the time I leave the clinic she feels real.

The train is crowded—I am pressed between a hoodied youth in black jeans and a white-collar guy with slicked hair. There's a hand on my arse. Curiously detached, I feel my curves through the stranger's palm.

***

SKIN

Later, as you watch, I strip down to my skin—shucking heels, Columbines, Kate Sylvester dress, push-up bra and panties. I climb into bed, tucking myself into your armpit. You turn off the lamp and your hand moves to my arse, stroking lightly. My world expands—I know what I look like through your hands.

Anonymous in a fiction of bricks

My city is held up by water. A ship drifts on the glassy image of buildings.

You wander the piers with a notebook—a man sweeps litter into a long-handled dustpan with a broom made from twigs—he wears a possum-fur hat and laced leather shoes with synthetic soles—he watches for flat mouths—he spends a long time on the pier staring at *Solace in the Wind*—he watches gulls.

A girl in a fur hood flirts with pigeons.

***

My city is held up by walls. Plaster marks grey scars on the old skin of paint.

I wait for lifts—they cough up consumptives into my breathable air—doors close on my line of sight—I am a cube of silver mirrors—breath condenses into scrawled messages of hope that resonate like you.

A woman, slick in black, wheels a bike into the foyer.

***

My city is held up by maps. A turn to the east is a turn to mist.

I take tracks to nondescript places—I sleep in defaced bunkers—I am scorched by lurid Picasso dreams—I am Harlequin in a concrete mirror—I wake reptilian.

A grizzled man with a crooked leg embarrasses traffic.

***

My city is held up by hills. Woolly humps fringed with ragged coast.

You are there—I am here—between us pavement, gravel, leaf litter, scree—pieces of rubber shed from my soles—soles stop our feet sharing stories with the road—a call from you means H-E-L-P—a call from you means somebody died—I get the hiccups—I can't sing hymns—I speak in semiquavers.

A dreadlocked man enfolds his dog in his lap and begs.

***

My city is held up by roots. Fine hairs grow quickly, tickle the earth's throat.

You dream in logic—your dreams are algebraic—x is where you are—sometimes in your dreams y is where you are—in your dreams i am an imaginary number.

A cropped woman leans into her laptop in a crowded café.

***

My city is held up by rock. Fractures run deep in the greywacke basement.

You talk in tonal corrugations—I'm easing into dips and lurches—I'm leaning into lies—I'm bracing myself against my bones—push me, see if I fall.

I unfurl in rubble.

Salutation

I caught a bus heading from Denver to Kansas City but disembarked hundreds of miles early in the middle of nowhere. I asked the gas station attendant for the key as instructed. He handed it over then pointed across the prairie to a speck in the distance.

"That's it over there," he said through a mouthful of gum. "Watch out for rattlers. Ain't no hospital 'round here."

I thanked him and stepped out onto the grassland. A crow circled overhead. I shivered. By the time I reached the house the sun had set. I unlocked the door and moonlight followed me in.

The room was empty except for a mattress on the floor and a battered poster lying in a corner. The poster was a knockoff of a Magritte painting—the one where a woman stands naked with hair flowing down her back and looks out to sea, a sliver of moon above her. I gripped onto it as if it would save me from vanishing into the void of the unknown house. The moon crept higher and at some point I slept.

At dawn I awoke and went outside to watch the moon slip away. I undressed, released my hair and lifted my arms to the rising sun. The cawing of the crow saluted me.

Perigee

It is a supermoon night. Erika is etched in silhouette, smoothed to monotone by sooty light, perched on the deck rail. Inside, you sit in a glimmer of moon. Your charcoal rasps the paper, quickly catching her shadows. You have many sketches of her back, but this, you think, may be the best.

The moon slips further along its arc and you now sit in gloom, watching. A morepork hoots and Erika turns her head. You reach for your charcoal, then stand, dropping it to the floor, and walk out to take her hand. The moon is only the moon.

Daughters of the air

Let me tie up your shoelaces and we'll walk. We can talk about how they've banned mermaid tails down at the Dunedin pools, or how bacon doesn't taste like bacon any more, or how I almost slipped through that hole in my pocket, forty years or so ago.

You'll remind me of our unmothered mother and I'll try again to mother you, like painting blue sky and bright stars on jail walls. I'll pick up your left hand and feel the face of Jesus in the scars on your palm. This time you might lace your fingers in mine for a small moment as if you know me.

We'll get to the beach and walk away from our shoes, pretend we're still beautiful. Sit, and I'll comb your hair like you were Waterhouse's mermaid. I'll tuck the comb into my pocket and it'll slip through the split lining to be lost in the thin-glazed shingle. A small boy and his mother looking for sea stars in rock pools will find it caught in the tails of kelp.

The underbellies of clouds will blaze. I'll shift my gaze from the horizon and find you tracing your lacework scars with a finger, as if the nail could re-spin the narrative in gold. The sun will melt onto the water like butter and we'll shiver as it seeps away.

It's time to go now, so let me tie up your shoelaces.

We walk, like stepping on blades; we try to talk, our tongues like stumps; you slip through that hole in my pocket and turn into sea foam.

SEVERANCE

The possum hunt

Yesterday my tree was heavy with the suede softness of peaches.

Last night you feasted, leaving only corrugated husks and tattered flesh on the ground. Somewhere you are folded around your swollen belly.

Now, I hunt. The bush sheds the dappled light of day and fades to moonshine-deep. Soon the night will come. I am wrapped in the warp and weft of dusky shadows, tracing the threads of your passage from one tōtara to another. My shoes are as silent as whispers. The grizzled silver ferns brush me lightly as I pass—dew-drizzled ghosts in the billowing mist of my breath.

Steaming pellets rest lightly on the leaf litter—a scatological signpost pointing northeast, and the dubstep of my heart trips into triple step. The scent of musk settles under the weight of my attention—heavy, gamy.

I am still. The bullets are restless.

Held fast

The clamour inside my head faded to a sigh a while ago. I count to pass the time: the car radio died on the 82nd beat of Billy Joel's 'Piano Man'; there were fifty-two random clicks of the engine as it cooled down; there are six chips of windscreen glass in front of me; my heart misses one in every twelve or thirteen beats.

My face is pressed to the road. The tarseal sweats an oily haze that sears the inner lining of my nostrils. Skirting the outer reaches of my sight is a dragonfly. The thrumming of its wings is louder than the pulse in my left ear. Now it hovers close enough to stir my lashes, and the wings are iridescent with refracted light, like oily puddles scattering rainbows. It lands beside my heated cheek, close enough for me to interrogate its pixelated eyes. The robotic mouthparts chatter to me for a moment, then the dragonfly raises its wings as if to fly, but the tar holds it fast. One tug at a time the dragonfly begins its juddering dance.

I pass the time, counting the beat.

Settlement

Where are the crosses? Where are the stones? Our bones have been loosed like runes; my father's femur lies crossed over mine.

I ride the bales high on the tractor tray. Daddy drives, half-turned in the seat. Sun and dust turn my eyes to firewater.

It rains on the wounded pūriri. It always rains. In the dank shade our exposed bones turn green. One femur has a spiral crack; its neck has been gnawed by rodent teeth.

Daddy hangs a swing in the rimu. He spins my smile more and more and more, until I can't right the world.

The pūriri is scarred with the calluses of ghost-moth burrows. A wētā huddles in an older, smoother hole.

Daddy holds me up to clean the trophy antlers with a duster. I used to fear the daddy-long-legs spiders when they were nameless.

Once an emaciated hound snuffled through the litter and took away one of my ribs, then returned for another.

Daddy comes to get me in his new Kingswood. I know Mummy's waving from the porch but I don't look back.

Time slips on its sprockets, skips from now to when and back again; am I fleshed or flayed? Am I me or memory?

We climb for a long time. I try to place my feet in Daddy's footprints—a game I can't win, but it helps me keep up. Water drips off the brim of Daddy's hat.

The litter around our bones twitches with life. Sometimes—when time lunges forward—violet, coral-like fungi explode from the compost.

Daddy talks of hallowed ground—special places like where the antlers appeared. We've gone off-track and onto an unmarked goat path. He says it's not far now.

Sometimes, when deer pass, my father's bones and mine catch and slip like tectonic plates.

Aren't caped crusaders bulletproof?

The day I walked into the Four Square and saw the balaclavaed man waving a gun at the owner, I hesitated. I swivelled back towards the door but stumbled in my getaway. The gun changed focus. The eyes behind the balaclava darted from me to the owner who was rummaging in the till and clattering coins into a paper bag.

I'm no caped crusader. My tights sit bunched up around my ankles, my cape is a wet-weather poncho and nothing is monogrammed—hasn't been since Mum sewed labels into my clothes so I could find them in the lost-and-found. I'm no Superman, nor Wonder Woman for that matter, although I did once hold an unlockable toilet door shut against three burly women trying to get in to snatch my purse.

No, I'm no caped crusader but that day something snapped. I grabbed the closest weapon—a bottle of 2017 Montana Chardonnay—and threw it like Thor throws his hammer. It landed at the thief's feet. Smashed open. The gun went off. As I fell, the scent of peach and apricot filtered through the room.

Leaving here

I drive north from Emporia, past the darkened roadhouses and the flashing signs of pay-by-the-hour motels, then west through the swamp to the coiled razor wire that marks the correctional center. I stop at the end of the blacktop. Lynyrd Skynyrd's 'Free Bird' is playing for you—the wailing of the lone guitar—as I walk the halls to your cell.

We sit. A cigarette hangs from your lips. Ash fills the ashtray. "It'll kill you," I say. The clock ticks like a death-watch beetle. Click. Click. Click.

We talk. Baseball. Books. Family. Funeral. I twitch, dammit, like the last spasms of a dying bird. You want us to be strong, ongoing. You pass me your last Marlboro. I don't smoke. You laugh and order six toasted cheese sandwiches, French fries, ketchup, six Cokes.

Click. Click. Click.

The Death Squad in black suits stand guard. "I bear you no ill will," you say, and we walk the short Walk. Six steps. We feel cheated—it should take eight. They strap you to a gurney. The phone rings. "No, this is the Death House." Wrong number.

Later, I get back on the blacktop and drive east, away from the razor wire, then south to Emporia, past the bright and busy roadhouses, listening to the wailing of the lone guitar on my radio.

Le jour du jugement—Toulon 1793

Judgement day and they're herding us like beasts through the arch in the city wall. I'm holding Geneviève, her face buried in my neck. Aveline walks with me, shoulder to shoulder, the baby silent on her hip.

"Don't worry," she says. "Papa died for their cause. We'll be safe."

I don't tell her safety is not hereditary.

The open field is heaving with people. The patriotic jury weaves through the crowd. I know them but they pretend we never shared a table, never discussed politics. One of them points at me. "You!"

"No!" Aveline grabs my arm.

"Don't protest," I tell her. I lower Geneviève to the ground and put her hand into Aveline's. "Stay safe."

My arms are wrenched behind my back. I manage to brush my lips against Aveline's before I'm dragged away. I look behind once but they are gone.

The jury forces me into a row of men extending the length of the field. The artillery is lined up in front of us. They load the shot. The wicks are lit. I close my eyes and pray to a god I abandoned long ago.

Serving a subpoena in the outback

A bat is corpsed—hangs off the chain-link gate by a wing-tip. My car galang-galangs over the cattle-stop like racketing cicadas. The homestead hides in the hot blur but the GPS tells me I'm on the right track.

***

The house, roof blooded by rust, hunkers on stumps. The man sits on the slumped verandah, waiting. His teeth don't have to bare themselves for me to know he's a hunter—the ragged fragments of flesh are there in his laughter as he takes the letter from my hand.

***

Flies stick to the corners of my eyes. Muscles squirm beneath my skin. Silt settles between my breasts.

The truth of it

After the darkest day when Zeus captured the sun then flung it back, red-clotted, onto the battlefield, Father made my mother promise to take us if he didn't return: through the gate next to the chapel, down the rocky, moss-covered steps, into the catacombs, along the tunnels, moist and dark, then through the mountains until we reached his brother's farm.

Mother nodded and kissed him fiercely.

But Tito said we would destroy the Achaeans. Our warriors were braver, our weapons superior. For the first time I let him share my bed. I clung to him and he promised to return.

The next day Mother bundled food and clothing into packs. I went to the viewing platform to watch the battle, wearing Father's colours on one arm and Tito's on the other.

Our men stood in formation waiting for a signal from Hector, warrior of warriors, hero of heroes. When it came, they surged forward. But the Achaeans were tiger-swift, their armour glistening, and, charging from their midst, a wild man.

Our front line trembled. Amid the frenzied stabbing, warriors lay groaning and the enemy drew closer to our city walls.

That night neither Tito nor Father returned. Mother refused to stay. I watched her lead the little ones through the gate and down the rocky, moss-covered steps, then I went to wait for my men.

But Father knew the truth of it. The city burned on a warm summer's night. In the aftermath I am forced to open my legs to one Achaean warrior and then another, until I crack like blackened stone.

The bridge on a rainy Tuesday night

James and I are in the back seat, laughing, sharing the bottle. I take another swig—the whiskey burns. I pass it over to Summer.

River has one hand on the wheel, the other moving rhythmically under Summer's dress. We are cocooned in his Mazda 6. Outside, rain drips down the window while we make an attack on midnight. River abandons Summer's lap, takes his turn at the bottle.

James reaches for it, slugs it down, passes it back to me.

River's hand is active again and Summer starts mewling. "Yeah, baby," he whispers.

Out the window, lights glow in the distance, studding the land with stars. Summer keens her crescendo.

The bottle floats in my hand. I undo my seatbelt and climb into James' lap. His mouth claims mine, whiskey-sweet, then trails an arc of sleeted fire down my neck. I fumble with his zip and we dive into the lure of shared passion.

I rest my lips on James' forehead and taste the sweat on his skin. He nudges me and nods at the front seat. I look over my shoulder. Summer's head is bobbing up and down in River's lap.

I nip James' ear. "Later," I say.

River's breath is laboured. "Wait!" he says. "Let me pull over."

Too late. He moans and the car shudders with his release. The whiskey bottle flies from my hand. I am thrown onto the cold ground. Above me is the bridge. Lights flicker in the distance. The lonely, lovely, fading lights.

A response to the poems 'Brooklyn Narcissus' (first published 1958) by Paul Blackburn, and 'Midnight with Bottle' (first published 2017) by Jac Jenkins.

Advance of the cane toads

Toad, I congratulate you on your success—how far you've advanced since the Bureau of Sugar Experiment Stations ushered you in, saluting your gluttony for the cane beetle that grubs their crops. Today your poison laps along an expanding western front, your loaded glands weapons of mass destruction. Even the death adder is defenceless against you. I commend you on your twenty-metre ladders of toxic eggs and your status as state icon of Queensland. You wait in cowpats for the dung beetles to come—I commend your patience.

But there's a man in town who euthanases your soldiers with HopStop. He knows how to hone and brandish a blade like Schwendeman—cuts them widthwise at the crotch, strips their skin (no cracks, no holes), dissects precisely round the poison glands. He salts and dyes gutted skin to fine leather, beads their eyes and seals their lips. Sews zips in the groin to make purple purses for the tourists' coins.

Saving Daisy

Henry saved me when I was seven. Ripped me from the ocean, threw me down on the sand, pounded my chest and forced air into my lungs until the ambulance came. He gave the police his name and me my life but he'd gone by the time I came around—I don't know if anyone thanked him.

Ewan tried to save me when I was fifteen. There's this street where all the uni students live—parties every night. No one asked if I belonged or how old I was—except Ewan. He'd suggest I go home, that my parents would be worried, but I shrugged him off. When I passed out or was too sick to resist, he carried me. After a year he just disappeared. My parents missed him.

Rachel found me at twenty-five. My right eye throbbed and I was screaming abuse at the departing customer who'd given me the shiner. She was on the game too but had it figured out better than I did. Perhaps it's because she wasn't as desperate, was using it only to make a quick buck to get back on her feet. We were together six months until she told me she'd made enough to leave her night job and focus on a nine-to-five. She wanted me to leave too. I couldn't.

Ollie came the closest to saving me after Henry. Ripped me off the street, threw me into a rehab centre, pounded me with God's word and forced me to look at myself. I didn't like what I saw and left before it was too late. Hooked my toes over the edge of a rail. Wavered for a moment, thinking about giving myself to God.

BREAKING: Powerful quake jolts Kermadecs

I spread the blanket on the sand, plastic-side down. You leap on it before I can straighten it, laughing at my scowl. You pat the rug, tartan-side up.

"Sit."

"I'm not a dog."

But I sit beside you faithfully, loyally. You take my hand and I rest my head on your shoulder. The moon lingers close to Rangitoto. It's not yet midnight but soon the air will be black. The sea laps contentedly, breathing in and out, in and out.

"So are you going to come?" you ask.

"Where?" But I know where.

"To the fight."

I don't say anything.

"Please."

"You fight like a baby and I hate seeing you lose."

"Do not!" But you laugh. You always lose and you always laugh.

The clouds are gathering. One skitters across the moon, throwing shadows on the water. And the sea murmurs, sighing in and out, in and out.

You'll ask until I say yes, that I'll go with you to the ring where it's legal to beat someone to a bloody pulp. "Let me think—"

But I can't finish. The moon sucks at the sea, swallows it. Water surges like a drunken fool on a Friday night. Like drunken fools we watch and wait.

And the sea heaves in ... and out.

Come with me to Dunkirk

We will stand unseen on the wide swathe of sand and watch the bodies float out to sea. The wind will whip up sea foam round our ankles while we wait. In the dunes a French soldier buries an English one, takes his dog tag, keeps his mouth shut. Later we will watch him die. There is no forgiving the innocent.

Come with me. We will stand unseen on the bow of a fishing boat manned by everyday heroes. We will watch courage desert the brave—good men will lose their minds. There is no saving the innocent.

Come. Stand with me unseen on the wing of a plane. Watch the pilot close his eyes, realise, to save lives he must take lives. Watch as he fires, time and again and again. Clears a path for the fishing boats. Sends an enemy plane spluttering into an oil-coated sea. Creates an inferno and kills more than he intends. There is no defending the innocent.

Stand unseen on the wide swathe of sand and watch the pilot land his fuel-less plane. Watch him destroy it. The enemy closes in, takes him. Turn to the ocean and watch the fishing boats loaded with broken soldiers disappear over the horizon. Watch the bodies of the dead undulate on the sea. There is no protecting the innocent once innocence has gone.

A response to the movie Dunkirk (2017) directed by Christopher Nolan.

Scales: An assimilation of Val Plumwood

"The eye of the crocodile ... is golden flecked, reptilian, beautiful. It has three eyelids. It appraises you coolly it seems, as if seldom impressed, as one who knows your measure." (Plumwood, 2012, p16)

PROLOGUE

I go too far. I always go too far.

Slowly, slowly the walls go up. I study each stone, its lichen, before I lay it in place. Some stones take days of thought. The house grows on the mountain by the plumwood trees, whose name I take for mine.

Some events are pivotal—the Lightning Man hurls his thunder in your direction and you can't see as you did before, before the sweeping flood.

BODY

I go too far into the Wet (I always go too far), too deep into crocodile country in my small red canoe. Crocodile eyes are flecked like fool's gold. They reflect my dumb astonishment as the canoe is struck by a snout.

Mid-leap to a paperbark tree, I am taken by the jaws, dragged into a whirling death-roll. The spinning finally stops—I find myself sucking air, still gripped by the crocodile, his teeth latched on my groin, resting. He pitches me into a second whirl of terror. Still I am not dead when the rolling stops again and he releases me into the mud beneath the paperbark tree. I pull myself into the tree and again the jaws grab, drag me by the thigh into a third roll in the black. I think, *This is so wrong—I am so much more than food.*

I am released into the mud, into the flailing climb, into life. I went too far, to the limit, and lived—a mangle of what I was before.

Epilogue

I write now, and think, in my stone house on the mountain. The previously abstract idea of myself as edible has become concrete. I am a luscious, nourishing food source—prey as much as a pig, wallaby, mouse or barramundi, and this is normal and how it should be.

Val Plumwood (1939-2008), Australian ecofeminist.

ELASTICITY

Stigmeology

My mother, a pug-breeder and amateur stigmeologist, showed me the space that can be held in punctuation—how we can exhale commas into chaos, settling a paragraph like a hound winding down around its tail to rest, nose propped on the basket's edge; how the question mark with its raised brow opens the eyes to that tock between two thoughts; how the full stop holds the tongue of the panting sentence against the next rush of unleashed sound.

My mother also said that flesh is a hyphen, holding soul to soil. My life with five pugs is a chaos of leashes.

The auburn trail

Cinnamon lived in a rambling house perched in that narrow space between city and bush that is neither one thing nor the other. Her father worked for an insurance company and was away for days at a time. Her mother stayed at home and wrote stories about the interconnectedness of life.

The largest room in their home was devoted to books. Many of them were written by her mother, some beautifully bound in hard covers with gold trim that Cinnamon would gaze at for hours. Others were paperbacks with screwed up corners and bent pages that Cinnamon devoured over and over. And there were the ones they fashioned together when no publisher would take them: spiral bound or in clear files or delicately held together with twine, the story carefully inked on hand-pressed paper.

Every morning Cinnamon and her mother sat on the window seat in the dining room. Her mother would brush out Cinnamon's long, thick hair until it shone like bronze, while Cinnamon listened to her mother's latest creations: stories of the land and skyscrapers, oceans and fountains, and on days her father was away, stories of untamed creatures and travelling salesmen. In the afternoons they would clamber over the back fence and wander between the pūriri and rimu or stop under a tōtara to listen to the call of a tūī or watch a pīwakawaka, tail spread, catching insects while the smell of leaf litter rolled around them.

One day her mother fell ill. The ambulance came and carried her away to a hospital in the city. Cinnamon sat on the window seat every morning, staring out at the spider web of streets sprawled before her, waiting for her mother to return. She visited once but her mother had dried up and all her stories had gone. Cinnamon couldn't go back. And her mother never came home.

Her father returned to work and Cinnamon was sent to live with her aunt, who looked so much like her mother that Cinnamon felt unable to breathe. Not many weeks later her father arrived to collect her, announcing he had found a live-in companion with two daughters to look after Cinnamon while he was away. They travelled back in silence along the winding roads that skirted the acres of untamed bush stretching between her aunt's house and their own.

Father's companion was an attractive woman with sleek black hair and hard eyes, and she was a little more familiar with Cinnamon's father than Cinnamon liked. The daughters were about Cinnamon's age, with cropped hair, sniggery voices and an obsessive interest in social media. Father bought them all smartphones and, while Cinnamon used hers for music and to text her father and aunt, the sisters used theirs to take photos of her mother's books, posting them online with scathing comments.

One morning Cinnamon sat alone on the window

seat, brushing out her hair, when her father's companion walked in.

"I hear there's a head lice outbreak at school," she said, producing a pair of scissors and brandishing them at Cinnamon.

The brush dropped from Cinnamon's hand and clattered to the floor. "No!"

The sisters grabbed her and held her tight while Father's companion snatched up hunks of hair and hacked at it. Long auburn strands tumbled to the floor.

"Much better," said Father's companion when she'd finished. "Now, tidy up this mess and get ready for school."

Cinnamon dropped to her knees and scooped up her hair, shoving it into her backpack while the sisters giggled and took photos on their smartphones. She pushed past them, snatched an apple and a muesli bar off the kitchen bench and left the house through the back door. A cool breeze soothed her burning cheeks and whispered over the top of her head, sending ripples through her shorn hair as she scrambled over the back fence.

"Cinnamon! Useless child. Where are you?"

"I think she's gone to school already, Mother," said one of the sisters.

Cinnamon crouched behind a pūriri and listened to their footsteps recede. She leaned back against the tree and sent a text to her father. Then she pulled the hair out of her bag and smoothed it into a silky pile on her lap. She searched through her pack until she had every last strand before fastening them together with a hair tie.

Her father's reply came a few hours later. *Don't be silly. Hair will grow. Home in 3 days.*

Three days! Gently, she placed her ponytail in her bag. She sent a text to her aunt, selected a playlist and stepped into the bush without looking back. Her phone died before her aunt replied.

The day grew dim and the cool dampness of the night bush seeped into her clothes. She shivered and wished she'd thought to bring a jacket. Settling herself under a ponga tree, she pulled her knees up to her chest, trying to extract as much warmth as she could from her body. A disturbance sounded in the undergrowth and one of her mother's stories rushed unbidden into her mind—it told of wild boars disturbed, of hunters and prey, of desperate animals guarding their offspring. She wondered if she had accidentally happened upon a den and turned around slowly. Four weka stared at her.

She laughed. "Look at you. And I thought you were a giant boar about to charge me."

Her stomach rumbled and she pulled out the muesli bar. The weka trotted closer.

"Are you hungry too?"

She divided the muesli bar into four and dished it

out. The weka ate from her fingers, their beaks tickling her skin. She munched on the apple but it did nothing to assuage her hunger.

"Well, little birds, I'm lost and hungry and very cold." She wrapped her arms around her legs. "I wish I had a nest I could snuggle into like you do."

They watched her, their heads cocked to one side.

"Aren't you going home?"

They gathered closer and spread their wings wide, wrapping them round her like a cloak. Her eyes filled with tears. She lay down and the weka snuggled beside her, covering her with their blanket of wings. Soon she was fast asleep.

She woke to sunlight sprinkling on her face and her stomach aching with hunger. The weka had gone but she could still feel their warmth against her skin. She reached for her pack. The zip was open and her once-ordered ponytail in disarray. "No!"

She snatched up her hair. The bundle felt lighter and she searched for the missing strands even though she suspected they were now lining a weka's nest. As she tucked what she could find into her bag, she noticed a flash of copper glistening in the growing sunlight. There, strung between two trees, hung a braid of woven hair.

Cinnamon followed the burnished strands as they swung from tree to tree, spun into intricate patterns that caught the filtered rays of the sun. One minute the strands were delicate and light but within a breath they became dense, absorbing the scattered light instead of reflecting it. Sometimes the strands spanned many branches, woven like the designs in a tukutuku panel; a step later a single strand hovered from one leaf to the next. Cinnamon felt as if her mother were with her, telling her a story of majestic trees and modest dwellings, of new life and old, of things misunderstood and freshly discovered.

The story stopped as the chill of evening settled in. Cinnamon drank from a stream, hunkered down in a small clearing for the night and welcomed the weka when they reappeared to keep her warm.

Cinnamon woke in the early light of dawn. Her bag lay open and once again strands of hair lay haphazardly around it—some in, some out and some weaving a story through the branches above her.

An army of orb-web spiders scuttled out of the trees, across the ground and over her leg. She leapt up, flinging her leg about until all the spiders had been thrown off. Above her, threads of hair wound their way between two rimu. A single spider shone like obsidian against the chestnut tones and reminded her of a tale her mother told of an ancient storyteller who could weave magic as intricate and delicate as a spider's web.

Cinnamon followed the spiders' trail to the edge of the

bush. To wide-open paddocks of rolling farmland. And in the distance, a road and a cottage. And outside the cottage a woman who looked so much like her mother that, once again, Cinnamon felt unable to breathe. Cinnamon's aunt lifted a hand and waved. Air gushed into Cinnamon's lungs with a force that sent her flying over the paddocks. The final strands of her hair billowed out of her bag and floated away on the breeze.

When plump berries fall

This tōtara tree is ornamented with tiny berries—gifts are quiet here, and if I hold my breath I hear the sap complaining at my pluck of fruit. "Tōtara here are like weeds," I whisper back. "This fertile earth won't miss a seed or two."

A thin trail of flattened grass leads to my feet. I watch bees move in to fill the space left by my passage through the paddock's clover flowers. Tōtara berries taste like guava. Though that's not what it says in the book of edible New Zealand plants.

I asked your father before the hush, "Could we make berry wine?" And here I am now, offering vinegar—redness splashing on the tōtara's spreading roots.

I don't believe in ghosts. That plosive stutter was simply a pheasant's urgent flight. If it were you, you'd be the sound of a small plump berry falling.

Your father's quad bike rumbles below me along the race.

Rationalists wear square hats

"You're late." The receptionist speaks to my shadow as she does every morning.

I ignore her and pause outside the meeting room. It's packed, the associates mildly distorted through sheet-glass walls. Jeff stands at the whiteboard red-faced, his arms flailing as he tries to explain our latest design. The managers look at the floor, at the ceiling, out the window—anywhere but at Jeff and his chaotic display. One of them notices me lurking and scowls.

Jeff shrugs as I open the door. He holds out the whiteboard pen. "Ava can explain it much better."

"You're late," my boss says.

I take the pen and survey the room: bored rationalists in square hats confining themselves, and us, to straight lines and right angles. I imagine them, not naked—too clichéd—but in sombreros dancing a mambo. I clear my throat.

"An old man sits in the shadow of a pine tree in China. He sees larkspur—"

"What the hell's larkspur?" someone mumbles.

"He sees larkspur, blue and white, at the edge of the shadow, move in the wind."

My boss coughs. "Come on, Ava, enough with all your Zen stories. The brief is clear."

I remember what he said on my first day. "So impressed with your freshness, your creativity." Clearly my freshness and creativity have outstayed their welcome.

"It's a poem, not a story. It says night is the colour of a woman's arm: obscure, fragrant, supple."

My boss opens his mouth and I speed past any interruption.

"It says that I can reach up to the sun with my eye and to the shore with my ear."

"Ava …"

I hold up my hand. "I'm almost done. It says the white folds of the moon's gown are filled with yellow light and its feet glow red, that one star shining through the grape leaves can carve more than knives and chisels."

Their faces are blank. They can't see the shimmer between blue and white, they can't hear the breeze swishing as soft as water flows, or taste the scent of night.

"It says that not one of you has the courage to think in rhomboids and cones. That you will never know the graceful journey of a line or that an ellipse holds promise. It asks you to wear sombreros but you won't."

Jeff is shaking his head at me. The room is silent. I collect my sombrero and leave.

Towards apostasy

Times like this, places like here, she feels like she is eating gravity—her belly expanding to hold the heavy silence. She is anklet-deep in still, peat-stained water. A listless bridge crosses the reedy creek to her right. Kahikatea infiltrate the water on all other sides—the pool is losing its edges, like her. She comes here, and places like here, to counter the hot pull of hedonism. A solitary penance of sorts, she supposes, although she lapsed long ago.

Her mother, loving her, grieves.

On the far side of the pool a sliver of dusk whittles itself from a trunk and takes on human shape—hard-edged and robust. The pool's surface ripples like tea-dyed silk for a moment. She feels examined, laid bare. Sweat crawls down her back.

She had touched him; rejoiced in him; tumbled into lust. Only her imagination—surely she has not fallen ...

She stumbles backwards out of the pool. The shape blurs into shadow and withdraws. Shivering, she puts on her sandals. Scum clings to the fine links of her anklet, but she leaves it be.

A friend will recommend toothpaste, and the silver will be resurrected.

She pauses on the top of the bridge and turns to look back over the reeds. There are ripples where she was standing, still.

My father bought an apple orchard

My birth certificate reads Benita Jackson. Tess says I used to be called Ben, but I've only ever known myself as Jo.

Tess is five years older than me and knows everything. She says I was a "difficult conception and a difficult birth". Because Mom and Dad couldn't have the son they wanted they named me after Grandpa Ben. Grandpa Ben ate apples to the stem, she told me. That's why he lived so long.

When I was six months old Uncle Joe died. According to Tess, that's when they changed my name to Jo.

Joe's death haunted Dad. One night he just up and left in the middle of a snowstorm. When I was older I asked Tess why. She said Grandpa Ben was wrong about apples and eating them whole hadn't helped Uncle Joe. But an apple never killed anyone—except Snow White and that doesn't count.

Every Christmas Dad sent a postcard and money. Mom threw the postcards away and spent the money on wine. Last Christmas he sent a postcard from Sterling, Massachusetts. He'd bought an apple orchard an hour out of Boston.

"See?" I said to Tess. "Dad wouldn't buy an apple orchard if apples killed Uncle Joe."

Today I'm eighteen. I jump off the back of the truck as it rumbles past the end of Dad's drive. It's close to midnight. He's sitting on his porch. Fireflies flicker and music spreads out into the night.

He splashes amber liquid into a tumbler and hands it over.

"Hello, Ben," he says.

A response to the poem Growing up (first published 2012) by Michelle Elvy.

Making our way home

The school bus regurgitates her at our gate and roars off, tossing us in a speckled cloud of dust. She stands on the roadside, dazed, eyes downcast, trying not to drown. I sense her internal fluttering—she is like a moth trapped in an ashen web, struggling with the fine strands of silk the day has woven around her. My day sits leaden on my shoulders and I don't have the patience to unravel her. She is halfway to the beach before I can say there isn't time, her bag a lump at my feet. I pick it up and follow.

The beach is littered with shells washed in with the tide: spotted whelks, golden limpets, southern olives, inky-black horns, and some so bashed and beaten by the surf they have no name. These are the ones she understands—their broken silence whispers to her and glues her together like a mosaic. The perfect ones she throws into the sea.

She sculpts a nest in the sand, scrape by scrape. I itch to shovel and scoop, to speed up time, but I have made that mistake before. She lowers herself into the sandy hollow. Waves lap over its rim and she hums to the beat of the ocean as she stares out to sea.

When the bottom edge of the sun dips into the water she clambers out of her salty chamber and we scramble over her newly uncharted rocks. Lost periwinkles unsettle her so she plucks them from their stony home and drops them into the water. In rock pools she lifts out starfish fallen from far-flung heavens, then lets the water settle before plunging them back in again.

Only a hint of gold stains the sky when she comes up for air. She offers me a tentative smile, then turns away quickly and heads for home.

The ghost of my father

The ghost of my father arrived at sundown. He was hunched over, carrying on his back a book so huge that at first I thought it was a slab of concrete. As he came nearer I could see *Lexicon of Theology* scrawled across the cover in black gothic lettering.

I'd been shooting rabbits from my chair on the porch and put down the gun. I rose to greet him. As he climbed the steps, memories of my childhood itched at the wall I'd built around them.

He stopped, offloaded his burden and opened it. From the middle pages gods of every religion oozed out. My father tore a branch off the wisteria growing along the railing and thrashed at them. They backed away. He tottered towards me like a child, offering the branch. I reached out.

Then I saw his hand—gnarled and claw-like, fingernails long and crusted with years of shame. I reached instead for the shotgun, took aim and fired. The book shattered into a thousand tiny pieces and the gods spiralled away towards the heavens, lighting the sky in a glorious display of colour. My father toppled down the steps and dissolved into the night.

In the end, freeing him was easy.

Mount Alpha

The scree rocks and slides beneath my feet. I am alone above the bushline.

I'm not alone above the bushline—over there sits a scruff-haired man with a scuffed sketchbook. He is engrossed and hasn't noticed me.

He notices me, looks up and then back to his pad. I have been dismissed. This is unusual—I am considered captivating. I tug off my beanie and toss my locks a little.

I cease tossing my hair—let the wind work its fingers instead. Step closer. He is eulogising eyebright and buttercup in ink.

He stops eulogising eyebright, scratches his nib coarsely across the page, cursing. Takes an old stem-winder from his pocket, consults it myopically. I can't wear a stem-winder.

I can wear a stem-winder but they always wind time down, one hour taking too long to pass. It's my magnetic field. My object of attention remains unaware of my magnetism, my tousled hair. He repockets his watch and tucks a heel under each thigh before leaning forward so his shoulders touch his knees.

His shoulders don't quite touch his knees, I see when I move closer still—he is not as yoga-flexible as me. He turns his head, although this is not recommended in his position. "What can I do for you?" he says.

I put on my beanie before my thoughts come spilling out.

A dog called Mana

The shopman named him Mana (a bit of a joke, for a scrawny, tufty shopdog) but now everyone calls him Minus (a bit of a joke, for a dog that lost a leg).

"Hello, Minus!" say the regulars who are popping in for milk or bread or smokes and still in their slippers.

"Pretty Minus!" says the skippety schoolgirl who is liberated by a small gold coin, hot in the palm of her hand.

"Hiya, Minus!" says the bearded man who parks under the disabled parking sign and gets his goods through his wound-down window.

"Howzit, Minus?" says the beer-bellied guy who asks for smokes on tick then ticks his family's bread instead.

"Hey Minus watcha been doin caught any sprats lately?" says the mad fisherman who spills the fuel as he fills his can down at the pump.

"Hi, Minus …" whispers the shadow-drawn woman who wraps herself in silence behind the sounds of the shop's radio.

"Attaboy, Minus," murmurs the shopman, who is counting lollies into lolly bags—ten for a dollar—as his dog walks by.

Mana has long since forgotten he once had four legs and he trots—*skip hiccup*—marking his own jaunty beat, and he has long since changed the minus to equals, and twice a day he casually cocks his one remaining hind leg on the disabled parking sign by the shop's front door.

The theory of elasticity

But there is one problem—how will Mum cope without me? I stare out the plane window. Mum will be on the observation deck, probably searching for her keys. I saw her put them in an outside pocket of her bag but she might have forgotten. I turn away and remind myself forgetting happens to everyone, or so Mum says.

When Dad died Mum was still lecturing in physics at Auckland University. They gave her six months' paid leave. It was the least they could do, they said. I noticed little things at first—they hardly seemed important. A lost word here or there, a small forgotten space in her day. A year after her return, the students complained about jumbled lectures that started too early or finished too late. The doctor said it was to be expected—she was still recovering. But the university gave her an early retirement package and let her go. She'd just turned 52.

Like Mum, I settled on physics for my degree and wanted to study in Auckland to be close to her. But she was adamant: "Absolutely not!" While there were other things she failed to recall, she'd never forgotten the treatment she'd received from the faculty.

So, here I am, the flight stretching the space between us. And I cry all the way to Wellington.

Her first call comes as I'm heading towards the baggage claim.

"Sweetheart, I've lost my car keys."

"Are you still at the airport?" I don't want to be right.

She laughs. "Silly, I've been home all day and I need to go to the supermarket."

"But I stocked up before I left."

There's a long pause. I tuck the phone into my shoulder, grab my luggage and head towards the check-in counter. The return flight hasn't been called yet and I might just make it.

"Mum, I'm coming home."

"What? No. I'm fine. I remember now. You're in Wellington and you did the shopping before you left. I've lost the car keys, that's all."

"Are they on the key rack?"

"Are what on the key rack?"

"The keys, Mum." I look up at the departure board. The flight back to Auckland is on its final call.

"Oh, yes, there they are. Thanks, honey. Bye."

I stare at the phone. I lose things too. And her bad days don't come that often. And a change of routine is bound to confuse her. And the Auckland flight has closed. I sigh, take one last look at the phone then head out to the bus stop.

I arrive at Cumberland House and, after dragging my suitcase down three wrong hallways, finally find my room. Small and airless, it squeezes me into the shape of a lost soul, but the other lost souls on my floor rescue me. They laugh too loudly, drink too much and study too little, pretending they aren't missing home. I pretend to play along, while

Mum tries to adjust without me. Her calls come every day.

"Honey, do you know where my blue scarf is?"

"Did you look in your top drawer? Right at the back." She only has one blue scarf and she hasn't worn it since the day the university fired her. I hope it's a sign she's finally moving on.

"Ah, yes, there it is."

"I've always liked that scarf, Mum. It's great you're wearing it again."

"Silly, I wear it all the time. It's the only one that goes with my floral blouse."

I don't tell her that the floral blouse hasn't been removed from her closet in almost three years for the same reason her scarf has been lying at the back of a drawer.

"Must dash," she says. "I'm taking Sarah to lunch to thank her for all her hard work."

Sarah lives down the road and has been helping us around the house since Dad died. Without her popping in once a week to do the cleaning, and at odd times to check in, I would never have come to Wellington. I smile and wonder if it's Mum taking Sarah to lunch or Sarah taking Mum.

"Okay, Mum, have fun."

My phone rings a week later when I'm walking to campus with a girl from my floor. The hill is a killer and we both stop. I pull my phone from my pocket.

"Is that your mum again?"

I nod.

She rolls her eyes. "Don't answer it."

"I have to. I'll meet you there."

She shakes her head at me and walks away. It hadn't taken long for the whole floor to notice that Mum phoned every day but I'm getting used to their ribbing—it's better than laying my life out in the open for everyone to see.

"Hi, Mum."

"Darling, do you think someone could have stolen my tablet?"

"Mum, you don't have a tablet."

"Yes, I do. You bought me one before you left."

"I bought one for myself and you used it once."

I wait. Let it sink in.

"Of course you did. You showed me ... what was it? One of those cat videos?"

"That's right." I look at my watch.

"I think I'd like a tablet. Perhaps you can get me one for my birthday."

"Perhaps." But I'm not sure I will—it's just another thing for her to lose. "I've got to go, Mum. The lecture's about to start."

Mondays are always the hardest—our floor doesn't sleep much in the weekend—but at least there are no morning lectures and I can get up late. My phone rings. I answer it with a groan.

"Sweetheart, my purse is missing."

"Have you checked your handbag?"

She has.

I yawn and rub my eyes. "Switch to Skype and I'll help look."

We hang up and soon resume our conversation on Skype. She hasn't turned her camera around and all I can see is the room lurching as she walks into the lounge. There's a vase of dead flowers on the coffee table.

"Mum, are you going to throw those flowers out?"

"No, there's still life in them."

The camera whizzes past a collection of brown petals and decaying leaves at the base of the vase. I can only imagine the smell. She moves to the kitchen. The benchtop is covered in dirty dishes.

"Where's Sarah? Shouldn't she be there today?"

"I fired her. Remember? I told you she stole my tablet."

"She didn't steal your tablet. You don't have a tablet. Mum, switch your camera round so I can see you."

Her face looms large on my screen. "Now I can't see you."

"Tap the camera icon on the screen."

"Oh, that's right." She giggles. "You told me that last time."

"It's not funny, Mum."

She scowls at me. Her hair hasn't been brushed and a flannelette collar slips into view.

"Are you still in your pyjamas?"

"Yes, and I can see you're still in yours so don't get so

high and mighty with me, young lady."

This time I do laugh. "Remember our pyjama days?"

She smiles. "Yes, and the movies we watched. And all that popcorn."

"Popcorn we were still finding under sofa cushions for weeks," I add.

There's a knock on the door and I follow Mum as she walks over and opens it.

"Sarah, what are you doing here? I fired you last week."

"You fire me every week, Jane." She thrusts her head at Mum's phone. "Is that you, Becca? How are you?"

"I'm fine, thanks, Sarah." And then, "Is Mum okay?" I mouth.

A slight frown mars her brow but it disappears quickly. "Your mum's fine, sweetie. Don't worry about her. Isn't that right, Jane?"

"I've lost my tablet."

"No, Mum, you've lost your purse." I put my phone on the bed and let them stare at the ceiling while I get dressed for class. "Do you think I should come home? Perhaps for the weekend?"

"Here it is!"

I pick up the phone. And Mum's waving her purse at the camera. "Sarah found it." She brings the camera up to her face. "Becca, honey, I'm okay." She sees my frown. "Really, I'm okay. Sometimes I forget things and sometimes I lose things but that's no reason for you to come home." She sounds lucid. Looks like Mum. And Sarah is smiling in the background and nodding.

Against my better judgement I agree to stay in Wellington.

As the weeks pass, our conversations become less about her forgetting and more about her remembering. Not the little things, like when I first started to walk, or my first word, or the time I fell off my bike, or the night I sobbed and sobbed because my first love had left me and she sobbed and sobbed because the university had let her go. No, we talk about the theory of elasticity, the laws of motion, Einstein and relativity, thermodynamics and the time she almost met Stephen Hawking. I learn more from her than my physics lecturer, who speaks to us as if we're still children. No one else notices, but when your mother has a PhD in cavity quantum electrodynamics and has always spoken to you as an adult it's hard to take him seriously.

During my physics mid-terms Mum phones again. "Darling, I've lost the car."

"Mum, I can't talk. I have to study. Royal Oak is small—you'll find it," I say.

"I'm not in Royal Oak, I'm in the city ..." She pauses and I hear a muffled conversation. "I'm at Starbucks on Queen Street."

"Okay." I have no idea how I'm going to help her find

the car. It's a nightmare finding parking in the city, let alone remembering where you parked. "Take the bus home. I'll get Sarah to help you look tomorrow." There are fewer towing companies than car parks and I hope it'll be collected overnight by one of them.

Mum is silent for a few seconds and then says, "Actually, I think I got the bus in." She pauses. "Yes, I did. I'm having lunch with Dad but I can't find his office."

My heart stops. And I can't breathe. And my voice catches in my throat. And I almost choke on my words.

"Mum." I swallow. "Mum, phone Sarah. Sarah will come to get you."

"But I've lost my phone. I'm using …" A mumbled question. "It's Bob's phone and I only know your number."

"Who's Bob?"

"He works here, I think." And I hear her ask. "Do you work here?"

She comes back to me. "Yes, he works here."

My throat burns. "Stay there. I'm getting Sarah."

I hang up. My fingers shake as I find her number. And I pray that she picks up. And I know what this means. And she agrees it isn't good. And she is on her way. I should be able to breathe again. But I can't, I can't. And the theory of elasticity swims in dark, stretchy waves in front of me. I am stretched so tight I think I might snap. I pull out my suitcase. Because there is only one problem. And physics can't fix it.

Slang

I wonder why I'm here, Slutwalk '13, Dunedin, walking in my daughter's stilettos. I feel like Jessica Rabbit, drawn bad. I hate heels—how they martyr my feet, how they mock my gracelessness, how they arch my spine in a parody of desire. One of the walkers wears a placard and nothing else. JESUS LOVES SLUTS. Sometimes her left nipple flicks out from behind. I glance to my right where my husband, who is not my daughter's father, keeps pace with us. He is here because *The Penguin Thesaurus of Slang* lists many more derogatory words for *woman* than *man*.

The ticket

When I won Lotto the boys insisted that, because they'd bought the ticket for my birthday, we should split the winnings three ways.

Henry took his share and went cruising in the Mediterranean, where he met a Portuguese model called Maria. They emailed from Lisbon for more money so he could bring her home to meet me.

Robert took Sally and the girls to Africa on an extended safari. When they came home they decided Jade and Lucy needed a private education.

"We don't have much left," said Robert. "You'll help out, won't you, Mum?"

And I did help—Henry and Maria as they flitted from country to country, and Robert and Sally with school fees.

"But surely you want to travel, Gran?" Jade said when we'd gathered for my birthday, ten years after the win.

"No, she doesn't," said Robert. "Besides, any money left she'll need for a retirement home. We must start thinking about that, Mum."

I ignored him. "I'd like to trek to Everest Base Camp."

"Cool," said Jade.

Robert laughed. "She's joking."

I'd never joked in my life.

Maria said, "Good of you, Mama Jill. Then come also to Portugal?"

Henry sniggered. "Not likely."

"Actually, I'd quite like to ride a donkey through the Grand Canyon," I said. "Europe doesn't really interest me."

The boys smirked and rolled their eyes.

Today I posted a letter to each of them from the airport. I might not be a comedian but the last laugh feels good.

Duchesses don't cry

When I was growing up I spent the summer holidays at my grandfather's bach with my cousins.

"Hello, Duchess," Pops would say, ruffling my hair when I arrived.

I didn't smile, but I'd stand taller and tilt my head just a little as a duchess would, glowing at being elevated to such lofty heights.

Every summer Pops took the oldest cousins fishing outside the harbour, to that magical place where I imagined fish jumping as the earth swallowed the moon, and the sun rose, gleaming, into a cloudless sky. I couldn't wait to go flying over silver seas in a tin-can boat, the wind whipping my hair about my face and the sting of salt in my eyes.

The year my turn came he tousled my hair then picked up his bag of bait. My nose crinkled at the smell.

"You don't want to come," he said. "It'll stink of dead fish. No place for a duchess."

Dry-eyed, I watched them leave while the moon hung heavy in the sky, speckling the tops of the ocean ripples with pinpricks of light. I was still standing there when they returned well after dawn, smiles wide. My grandfather lined my cousins up with their fish, and his camera snapped.

He turned it on me. "Smile, Duchess."

I didn't. Instead I blinked and tilted my head, just a little.

Thin places

I have a friend as fragile as glass. Even her words are splinters. I tweeze them from my skin and dab at the buds of blood. Scars are blooming on my arms. I pull down my sleeves and no one knows.

She hears death in her merlot. She tells me that it makes a slamming sound loud enough to knock the crystal from the shelves. I sweep it out the back door while she sleeps.

On Tuesdays we play pool at the local. The tables are stained and the felt is shiny with use. We put our coin in the slot and retrieve fourteen or fifteen balls. A quick flick of her eyebrows and the barman rushes to open up the table. Most of the time she wins.

Other nights she slips on a red sleeveless sheath and wrap-strap stilettos, and goes out without me.

Sometimes she rocks on her porch swing in the sun, broken, flaring prismatic light. I'm on the slat chair, leaning forward, evangelising *The Secret*. She spits out her response. Her venom burns.

I don't know which hurts me most—the bleeding, the sweeping, the losing, the burning. But it's the gusts of wind at the door that stop me from sleeping.

Use three-dimensional characters

Joe was as two-dimensional as a Picasso linoleum cut—flamboyant certainly, but flat. He folded into creases when he sat. You could do a three-sixty around him and twice in the circuit he'd become a vertical line.

Joe dressed in paper like a paper doll, his clothes tabbed at the shoulders and hips—he was a sharp dresser, but vintage. Unlike Ken he lacked a manly bulge, but made up for it with his trapezoid torso.

Joe spoke in bubbled speech, cutting and dry-witted. Erudite, but his words lacked depth. His snores spelled *purr* when he slept. You could tear his proposals to pieces, leave them scattered on the floor like litter.

Joe could slip under a locked door when the gun-packing villain had the only key in his pocket. He was a skilled shadower of suspects. Sadly, he was easy to counterfeit by Xerox. He often flew by origami but preferred planes.

Joe could fold himself in half seven times—become a solid cube, act out of character but never out of choice and only for a chapter.

***

Joe died by guillotine.

Notes

The Edgar Allan Poe quote is from his poem 'Ulalume' (first published 1847).

The poem referenced in 'Tulips and Chimneys' is 'Songs: III' (first published 1923) by E. E. Cummings. E. E. Cummings' name is capitalised in accordance with the *Chicago Manual of Style* guidelines.

'Virtuose' was developed from a poem that was written by the author under the guidance of Sue Wootton as part of mentorship provided by Creative New Zealand and the New Zealand Society of Authors (PEN NZ Inc.) Te Puni Kaituhi o Aotearoa.

'Daughters of the Air' is titled after Hans Christian Andersen's original working title for 'The Little Mermaid' and borrows a line from the poem 'Departure Lounge' (first published 2011) by Kate McKinstry.

Val Plumwood's quote in 'Scales' is from 'Meeting the Predator', in *The Eye of the Crocodile* (2012, Canberra, Australia: ANU Press).

The poem referenced in 'Rationalists Wear Square Hats' is 'Six Significant Landscapes' (first published 1916) by Wallace Stevens.

An earlier version of 'Towards Apostasy' was part of a collaborative work, 'In the Forest, by the Stream / Shade', written in conjunction with Alistair Tulett for NorthWrite's 2013 Collaborative Competition.

Versions of some pieces have been previously published in periodicals, anthologies, blogs and websites as listed below:

Blog Carnival 4: Flash Across Borders
    (NZ, Germany, 2012)
        'While the Moon Howls' (published as 'I was I')

Bonsai: Best Small Stories from Aotearoa New Zealand
    (NZ, 2018)
        'The Possum Hunt'

Fast Fibres (NZ, 2014)
        'Staying in Bed' (published as the poem 'Awakening')

Flash Frontier: An Adventure in Short Fiction
    (NZ, 2012-2019)
        'Sunrise' (published as 'Leaving')
        'Pōhutukawa' (published as 'Crimson Tears')
        'Tulips and Chimneys'
        'Coffee Date'

'Joel's Knickers'
'Virtuose'
'Salutation' (published as 'Inside Out')
'The Possum Hunt'
'Settlement'
'Aren't Caped Crusaders Bulletproof?'
    (published as 'Caped Crusader')
'Held Fast'
'Leaving Here'
'When Plump Berries Fall' (published as 'Fallen')
'My Father Bought an Apple Orchard'
    (published as 'Grandpa Ben')
'The Ghost of my Father'
'Mount Alpha'
'The Ticket'
'Duchesses Don't Cry'
    (published as 'Reflections of a Duchess')
'Thin Places'
'Use Three-dimensional Characters'

Micro Madness | National Flash Fiction Day
New Zealand (NZ)
   'Stigmeology'

Northern Advocate (NZ, 2005)
    'A Dog Called Mana' (published as the
        poem 'Mana')

NorthWrite 2013 (NZ)
    'Towards Apostasy' (published as 'Shade')

takahē magazine 92 (NZ, 2018)
    'The Auburn Trail'

Take Flight 3 (NZ, 2013)
    'Yellow'

Acknowledgements

Our thanks to Alistair Tulett, Anne Jenkins and Rebecca Reader for draft reading and helpful suggestions. To Janice Marriott whose enormously valuable critique pushed us into rethinking the structure—the volume is so much better for it. And to Michelle Cumber and Lesley Marshall who carefully attended to the nitty-gritty.

Thank you to Jac. I know I have suggested in the past that all the writing genes should be in one of us (me!) but if they weren't split we would never have created this rich volume of small pieces. It has been an absolute blast working with you and I can't wait for us to move onto our next project together. *Kathy*.

Thanks also to Kathy. Even though all the writing genes ended up in me it's been great pretending they were evenly split. Like how Santa Claus isn't true but it's fun pretending he is. Seriously though, I can't imagine a better person to collaborate with on such a project. Your astuteness, drive and patience kept me in line and on track—not an easy task, and you did it with flair. *Jac*.

Kathy and Jac grew up on a dairy farm near Maungatapere, New Zealand. They both now live in the Far North, where Jac's chickens pretend they are poets, and Kathy's cat's attempts at writing are promptly deleted. Both graduated with Master's degrees in creative writing within twelve months of each other and their work has appeared in various periodicals, anthologies, blogs and websites. This is their first collection.